For Ste xx

First American edition published in 2002
by Carolrhoda Books, Inc.

Published by arrangement with Oxford University Press, Oxford, England.

Text and illustration © 2001 by Joanne Partis

Joanne Partis has asserted her moral right to be
known as the author of the work.

Carolrhoda Books, Inc., a division of Lerner Publishing Group
241 First Avenue North, Minneapolis, MN 55401 U.S.A.

Website address: www.lernerbooks.com

Library of Congress Cataloging-in-Publication Data

Partis, Joanne.
    Stripe's Naughty Sister / by Joanne Partis.
        p.   cm.
Summary: Stripe's mischievous little sister leads him into prickly
cactuses and a muddy swamp before he finally has to rescue her
from a dangerously high tree limb.
    ISBN 0-87614-466-0 (lib bdg : alk. paper)
    [1. Brothers and sisters – Fiction. 2. Tigers – Fiction.] I. Title.
PZ7.P2565 Stf   2002
[E] – dc21   00-012363

Printed in Malaysia

1 2 3 4 5 6 – OS – 07 06 05 04 03 02

Stripe's Naughty Sister

Joanne Partis

🌿 CAROLRHODA BOOKS, INC., MINNEAPOLIS

Stripe wanted to play with his friends, but instead he had to look after his naughty little sister.

"Play with me!" she said.
"No," said Stripe. If he couldn't play with
his friends, he would just doze in the sun.
But the moment his back was turned...

. . . his little sister disappeared.
Stripe would be in big trouble
if he didn't find her. He had to catch
her before she went too far away.

Oh no! Stripe's sister ran into a patch of prickly cactuses. But she was small, so she easily walked between them.

Stripe was bigger. It was hard for him to squeeze between the spiky plants.

Ouch!

Stripe heard giggling and looked up—just in time to see his sister running off again.

Stripe caught up. He saw his little
sister grab a vine and swing
across a muddy swamp.

Stripe wasn't happy, but
he had to follow her.

The vine creaked and. . .

...gloop!

Stripe splashed into the swamp.

Stripe's sister was having a lovely time. She found a hollow tree and dived inside to explore.

Stripe caught up, but he was too big for the hole.
Thud! He bumped his head.

Stripe saw his sister perched on a high branch of the tree, but he had followed her enough.

"I'm prickly, and I'm muddy, and I'm sore," he said, "and I'm going home."

Behind him, Stripe could hear squeaking.
He tried not to notice it.
At last, he looked back.
His sister was still up in the tree.

"I'm stuck!" she cried.

Stripe knew he couldn't leave her.
He knew what a big brother must do.

Carefully, he climbed the tree.

He climbed higher and higher until he reached his little sister.

Now they were both stuck. Stripe didn't know how to get down. Then, he heard a CRACKING noise and...

. . . down, down, down

they fell.

Oomph!

Stripe's little sister landed on top of him—hard!

"Thank you for helping me get down.
You are the best brother in the world," she said.
And she licked his nose.

Stripe felt proud. They set off for home. And that night, tired after their adventures, they curled up together and fell sound asleep.